K836s

BOOKS BY E. L. KONIGSBURG

*Jennifer, Hecate, Macbeth, William McKinley,
and Me, Elizabeth*
From the Mixed-up Files of Mrs. Basil E. Frankweiler
About the B'Nai Bagels
(George)
Altogether, One at a Time
A Proud Taste for Scarlet and Miniver
The Dragon in the Ghetto Caper
The Second Mrs. Giaconda
Father's Arcane Daughter
Throwing Shadows
Journey to an 800 Number
Up from Jericho Tel
Samuel Todd's Book of Great Colors

SAMUEL TODD'S BOOK OF GREAT COLORS

written and illustrated by

E. L. KONIGSBURG

A JEAN KARL BOOK

ATHENEUM   1990   NEW YORK

*Samuel Todd and Laine dedicate this book
to the Konigsburgs: Amy E., Anna F., and Sarah L.,
with* ♥ ★

*Special thanks to Elsie Todd,
for without her wonderful photographs,
we would see much less of Sam.*

★See the great color *red*.

In my book, the great colors come in this order:

ORANGE
GREEN
PURPLE
YELLOW
BROWN
RED
BLUE
GRAY
PINK
BLACK AND WHITE

A pumpkin is all orange,
but not all orange
is a pumpkin.

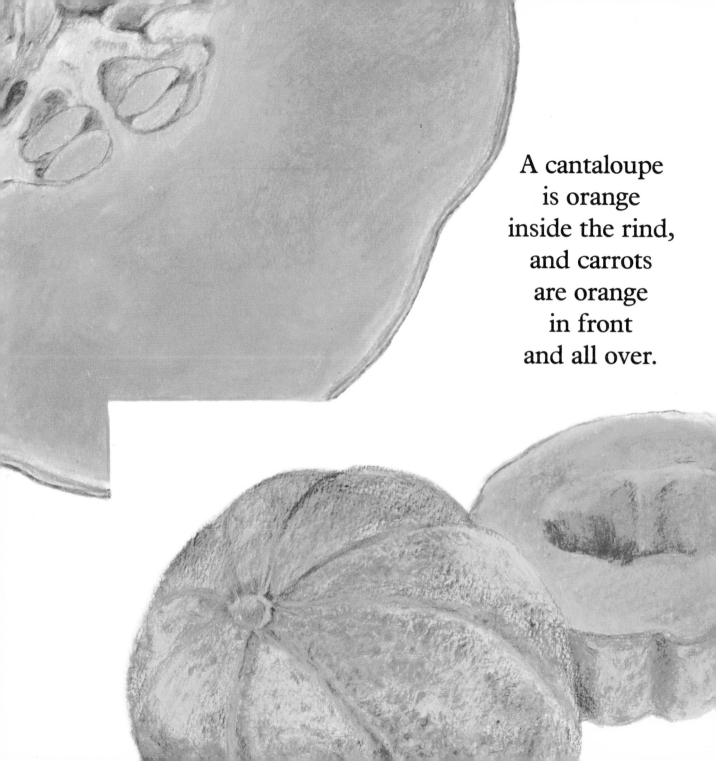

A cantaloupe
is orange
inside the rind,
and carrots
are orange
in front
and all over.

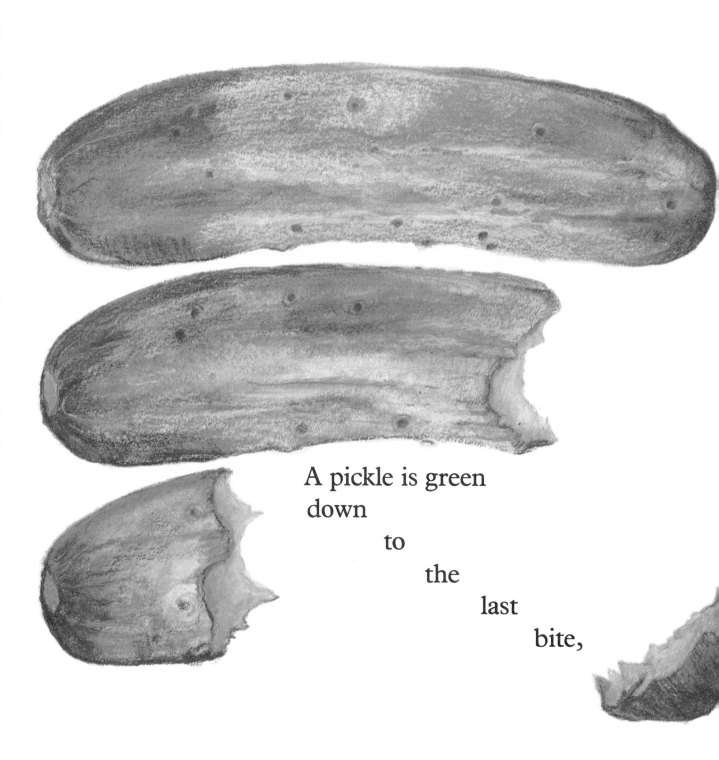

A pickle is green
down
      to
          the
              last
                  bite,

and so is spinach.

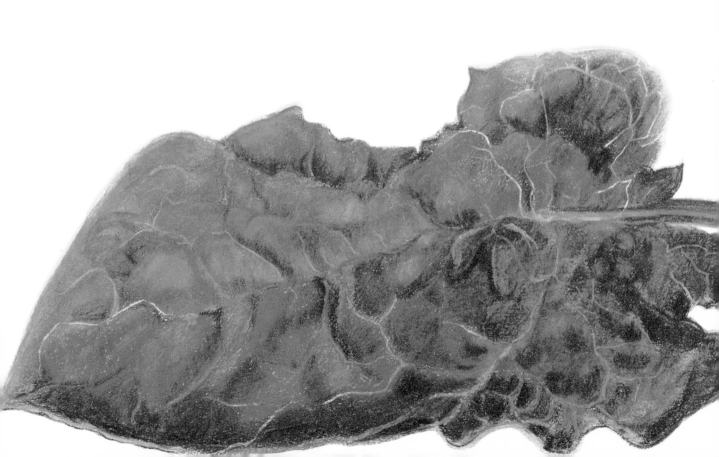

Eggplants are
purple,

and egg yolks are yellow.

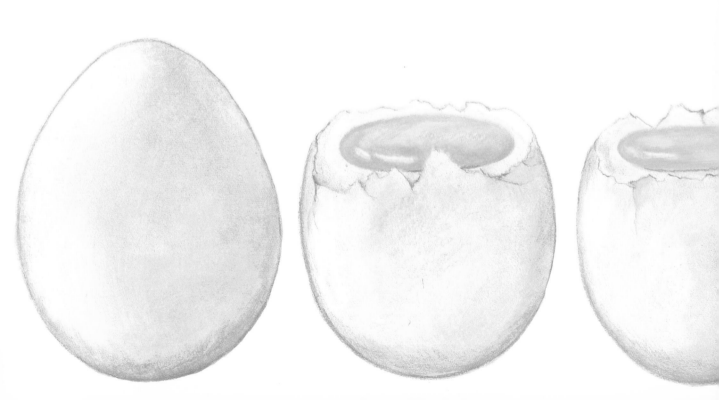

So are bananas.
Except for the speckles,
which are brown

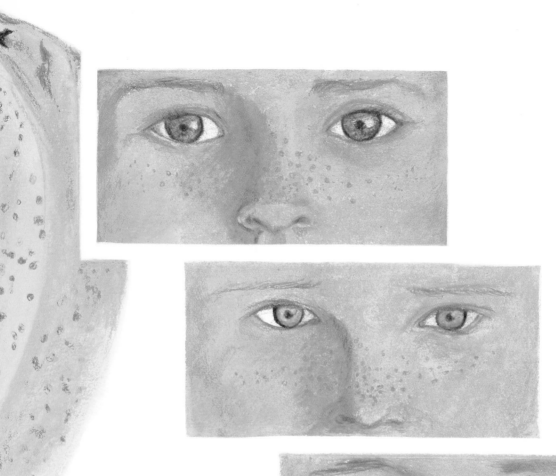

like freckles

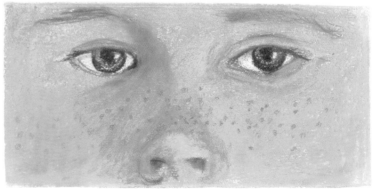

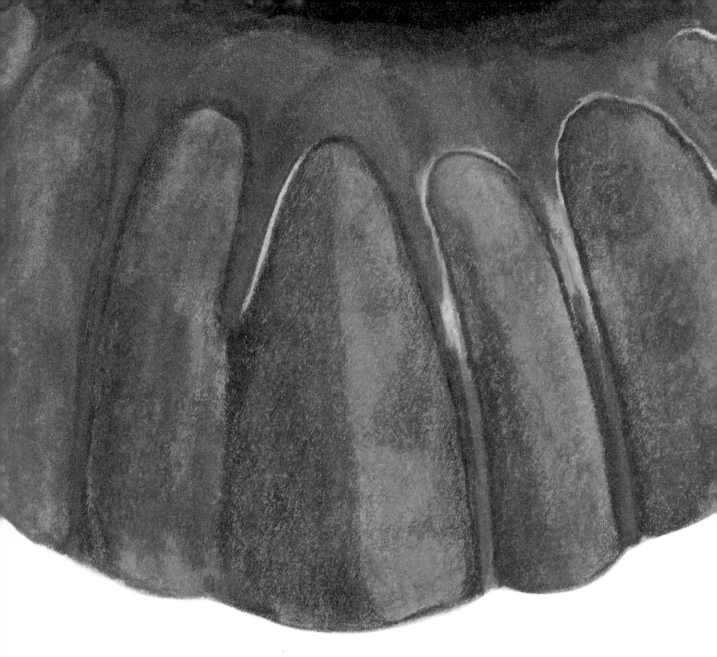

and chocolate!

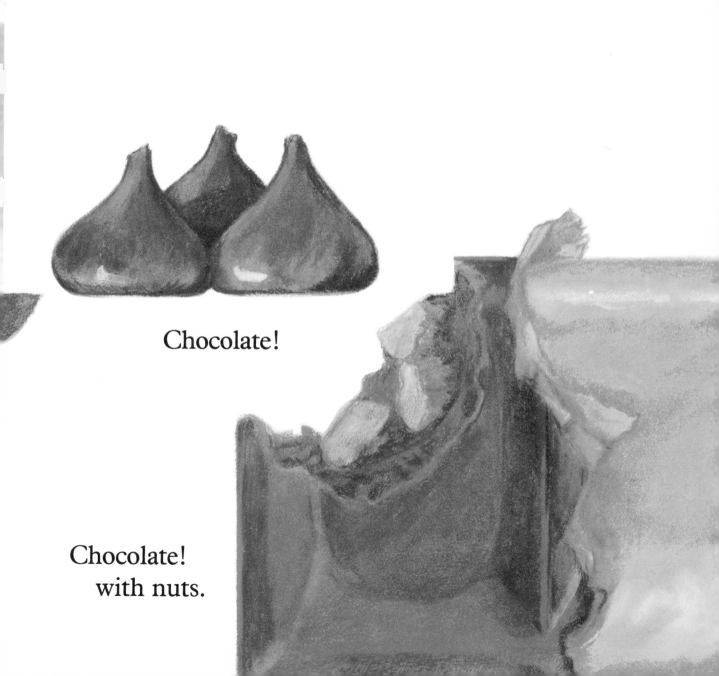

Chocolate!

Chocolate!
with nuts.

Hearts that say
LOVE
are red.

Be My Valentine

I ♥ NY

I ♥ Cocker Spaniels

Blueberries and blue jays are blue,
and that is why
they aren't called
yellowberries and
orange jays.

When you see a lot of gray
shaped like an elephant,
it is one.

Pink is for little girls, they say,
unless they know about flamingos.

Boy flamingos
are just as pink
as girl flamingos—
and in all the same places.

Pandas have black-
and-white faces.

Zebras are black
and white from
tops to bottoms.

Some
things
can
be
any
great
color,

and some have
no great color at all.
Like hugs and kisses and songs.
And they are some of the
best things of all.

Wrong: Kisses are pink.

Atheneum
Macmillan Publishing Company
866 Third Avenue, New York, NY 10022
Collier Macmillan Canada, Inc.
First Edition
Printed in U.S.A. by Horowitz/Rae
10   9   8   7   6   5   4   3   2   1

Library of Congress Cataloging-in-Publication Data
Konigsburg, E. L.
Samuel Todd's book of great colors / written and illustrated by
E. L. Konigsburg.—1st ed.   p.   cm.
Summary: Brief text and illustrations introduce a variety of
colors and where they may be seen, alone or in combinations.
ISBN 0-689-31593-7
1. Color—Juvenile literature.   [1. Color.]   I. Title.
QC495.5.K65 1990
535.6—dc20
89-6640   CIP   AC